You Can't Hate Me

Haters To genuine Lovers Romance

Marilyn R. Berry

Contents

Chapter One

It was fiercely pouring, consequently, students from the Baverly High School couldn't go out for a break. Some youngsters congregated around their mates' tables, gisting while others went to the library to read.

Sandra with her two besties; Lilian and Linda decided to go to the cafeteria, not only to eat but to gist as well. They opted to go to the cafeteria since it was quite huge, elegant, and busy. They went out of the class with their noses up as if they scented something terrible.

"Good afternoon seniors" a junior student hailed as he rushed by them, after a female who was sprinting eagerly. She was enjoying the pursuit.

"How nice it is to be named seniors and in the top class" Lilian commented as they entered the cafeteria

"Yeah, it feels so fantastic to be called senior, exactly like we did to others when we were juniors" Linda replied, attempting to keep pace with Sandra and Lilian who were going extremely rapidly.

When they eventually reached the cafeteria, they ordered snacks and beverages, brought everything to a tastefully furnished table in a corner, and sat down to eat.

"Sandra you've been silent all along and you ain't looking cheerful, what's wrong?" Linda inquired, examining Sandra who was playing with her ball pen.

"He believes he can tamper with me and go scot-free. No, he won't! I'm going to give him a lesson he'll never forget in a hurry!" Sandra replied, glancing at the flower that was positioned in the center of their table.

"Who the heck is he, Sandra?" Linda asked.

"It's the same son of a bitch who humiliated Sandra last week," Lilian said.

"You mean William, the class bully?" Linda asked in disdain.

"Yeah, it's him. He came into the class this morning with his dumb cronies and purposefully knocked on Sandra's table as he went by and the doughnut she arrived with slipped out and rolled everywhere as her bag shattered on the floor.

Everyone laughed at Sandra, even William and his ugly girlfriend, Lydia. He couldn't even say sorry, he simply laughed and went to his seat!

I felt bad for Sandra, I had to go soothe and assist pack her books off the floor. I wanted you to come sooner, but you're so accustomed to arriving late to school." Lilian explained.

"So sorry about that, Sandra. Poor you! You could've reported him or shouted at him for doing such" Linda stated

"I wanted to, I simply didn't know the correct words to employ. But not to worry, I'll give him a t-o-u-g-h lesson of his life" Sandra stated, smoothening the collar of her well-pressed shirt.

They were still chatting when William and his four buddies strolled into the cafeteria and sat down at another corner and started to speak and laugh.

What are you intending to do?' Lilian asked as Sandra stood up suddenly

"Watch me" Sandra replied sweetly and proceeded to where William and his pals sat.

She purposefully knocked into a student who was about to walk by William's table with a plate of apple juice and it occurred so swiftly.

The whole content of the juice fell and poured on William, from head to toe.

"Oops! What a disaster! Try and be cautious next time" Sandra replied mockingly to William and walked away, keeping her nose high up.

Everyone started laughing at William who was now begging for the earth to open and swallow him up due to the shame.

His buddies restrained the impulse to laugh as he rose and raced to the restroom to wipe himself off.

***

"That was very courageous of you" Lilian exclaimed to Sandra on their walk home after school.

"I never realized you were a genius, not only in emerging first every term in class but in revenging as well" Linda added, beaming at Sandra as they all walked out of the school grounds.

"William compelled me to do what I did. I wanted to show him that I may be a female, but I'm not a coward.

He can't keep embarrassing me and getting away with it. The other day, he splashed water on my uniform, and instead of saying sorry, he mocked me. I bet he'll never try me again" Sandra said proudly.

Did Sandra do the right thing by revenging William or did she just gets herself into big trouble?

Chapter Two

"I bet he'll never try me again" Sandra stated triumphantly.

Lilian and Linda's drivers were already outside the school compound, waiting for them.

They knew they had to part. They embraced and waved Sandra farewell as they hopped into their separate vehicles and the drivers drove off.

Sandra started to walk home slowly, heaving a sigh and thanking God that her house wasn't far from school, but she knew she would've still trekked even if it was far. Since her father died, it hadn't been easy for her mother to raise her all alone

Her mother, Suzan had taken up every menial job she could including washing peoples' clothing and cleaning up their homes simply to be paid so that she could take care of Sandra and provide her a better life.

She abandoned the cleaning job after she was nearly raped by a married guy whom she went to work for.

After washing and cleaning up his home, one day, the guy requested her to come inside his room and retrieve her money.

Though she wasn't comfortable with it, she summoned the confidence and entered the room.

Instead of giving her the money, he started rubbing her shoulders and telling her he would love to have a taste of her before handing her the money she worked for.

She felt irritated and simply told him she couldn't do such. He forcefully dragged her to the bed and was about to rape her when his wife came in and blamed Sandra's mother for seducing her husband into sleeping with her.

Despite her explanation, the angry woman didn't believe her. She was embarrassed and sent away without being paid.

Since then, Suzan had vowed never to take such work again. She started frying doughnuts which she displayed in a show glass and sampled outside her tiny compound.

At first, the sales were dismal, but as time went on people started trooping in to purchase it. Sandra of course took it to school to sell as well.

Sandra remembered how life had been when her father was still alive. He was a tall and handsome man who was very hard working.

He worked as a teacher in one of the biggest schools in town. His wife, Suzan had relied on his earnings because she wasn't working.

She hadn't been to College after high school, so her parents couldn't afford it.

Sandra's father had promised to give his wife and daughter a better life, not until he was crushed to death by a careless driver on his way back from work, on a cool evening, five years ago.

The picture of her father kept flashing in her mind as she walked home from school.

She had promised herself to take good care of her mother and make her proud. She kept her commitments by reading tirelessly and becoming the top in class since she joined Baverly High School.

Then her thoughts strayed from her late father to William, the class bully who had gotten terrible by the day.

He appeared to dislike her in particular, and she didn't know why. Or maybe it was because, unlike other students, she was the only one who was never terrified of him and would always find a way of getting back at him each time he humiliated her.

William on the other hand would stop at nothing to make her feel inferior.

He was no doubt the most handsome guy in school, had the richest parents, and lived in the biggest and most beautiful house in town, but that would never make her let him intimidate her in any way, never!

Yes, he was very intelligent. He was the most intelligent of all the guys in her class and that was why he had followers, had the most beautiful girlfriend, Lydia, and had his ways of intimidating people to get what he wanted, but no way! He wasn't going to do that to her, she was ready for him, she told herself.

Sandra eventually went home and discovered her mum working.

"Mum good day" Sandra welcomed. She walked to her mother who was arranging the doughnuts she had fried into a show glass and was about to take them outside to sample.

She embraced her mother who smelled of smoke because of the doughnuts she'd been cooking.

"My daughter, my pride, how was school today?" Suzan questioned, gazing at her eighteen years old daughter who was now so tall and gorgeous that she wished her late husband was there to see her.

"It was a busy mother," Sandra said, apparently fatigued from the journey.

"So sad about that baby. I prepared your favorite dish. Go in, freshen up, eat and sleep so that you'll wake up and study" Suzan said, patting Sandra softly.

"No mother. After eating, I'm coming back to assist you with what you're doing. I can't let you worry yourself while I'm here" Sandra said.

"But you must be exhausted after walking down to school and trekking home. I wish I had enough money, I wouldn't let you trek, I'd hire a driver for you" Suzan stated soberly.

"Mum stop saying that, I'm not complaining, I enjoy the trek. I insist on helping you, and that's final" Sandra said and ran inside.

"Such a nice youngster" Suzan murmured as she brought the display glass outdoors.

Sandra went to her immaculate room, a modest refuge, dumped her stuff, and bathed. She eventually joined her mother outdoors as she promised.

***

You believe you've won huh? You think you can meddle with a viper and get away with it?" William stated pinning Sandra roughly against the wall.

How long will William continue to torment Sandra?

Chapter Three

"You believe you've won huh? You think you can meddle with a viper and get away with it?" William stated, pushing Sandra forcibly against the wall adjacent to her locker the following day in school when everyone had gone outside for sport.

"Let me go! You horrible bully! I'm not terrified of you! I detest you!" Sandra muttered, attempting to pull William's hands off her, but he'd grabbed her so tightly that she couldn't move.

"You don't need to tell me you hate me, because I hate you more and I'd hate you forever! Do you know why? Because you're darn obstinate!

I get whatever I desire! No one dares to challenge me, but you have always attempted to cross my path and dare me, and I guarantee you, when I'm done with you, you'll repent the day you stepped your filthy legs into this school" William growled, digging his fingers into Sandra's neck until she started gasping for air.

Her eyes were wide. She felt her breath leaving her and her legs losing balance and sinking slowly to the earth.

"William, a teacher's coming" One of his pals who were on the watch out notified him and he swiftly let go of Sandra who dropped like a piece of wood on the floor and was panting as if she had run a 400-meter sprint.

William devilishly winked at her and went away.

***

"Sandra, where have you been? We've been looking everywhere for you. You know you're the only one who can volley well on our team and we lost the game because you weren't there" Linda and Lilian exclaimed as they came in and spotted Sandra sitting all alone in the empty class.

Getting to her seat, they discovered that girl was weeping.

"Sandra, what's the matter? Why are you crying? Is your mother alright? Is she ill again?" Lilian inquired as Linda reached out to wipe Sandra's face.

"Mum's alright" Sandra answered softly.

"Then what's the matter," Linda asked, pulling her gently to herself.

"It's William. I don't know why he dislikes me so much. What have I done to him that he keeps hurting me?

He pinned me to the wall, hurting my throat. I couldn't breathe. I almost died" Sandra said painfully.

"This isn't funny anymore, it's getting out of hand. I think it's high time you reported him to Principal Sarah! She could call and give him a stern warning to stop bullying you" Lilian suggested.

"I won't do that! He'll call me a coward. I'm a big girl, I'm capable of handling him" Sandra said, suddenly brightening up to the amazement of Lilian and Linda.

"Ain't you terrified of him? Don't you believe he'll do something more detrimental to you whenever he gets the opportunity?" Linda asked, concerned.

"I'm equal to the task. I'll deal with him. I'll so deal with him. I know what to do, trust me" Sandra replied with a strong expression that made her appear even more lovely.

***

"Mum, tell me you're joking me. Tell me you ain't traveling again!" William stated, stepping into the huge sitting room where his mother was standing, after making several phone calls.

The property was really huge and exceedingly gorgeous with a great lawn and swimming pool outside.

His father, Mr. David, actually invested a lot in creating the home. He was one of the wealthiest business guys in town.

His mother, Felicia, was a lovely lady who appreciated refined things. William looked precisely like his mother; tall, black, and influential.

He was capable of making things work out in his way.
William has always grumbled that his parents never cared about him since they traveled virtually every day.

"Yeah baby, your dad and I are traveling this afternoon.
It's a business trip and we just can't miss it, I'm sorry. But not to worry, I'll transfer a hundred..." His mother started, but he interrupted her.

"You believe money is everything? I'm weary of your blasted money! When was the last time you asked me how I was doing at school?

When was the last time you bothered to know how I was doing at all?

All you do is travel, keep massive quantities of money and tell me to have fun.
I'm sick and weary of this entire affair" William replied fiercely

"William, don't start again. You know we care about you and we're doing all this for you, so that when we're no more, you'll take over and enjoy a stress-free existence" Felicia replied gently.

"Stress-free life? You know what? Go on! Go anywhere you want to go, I don't care!" William said and stormed out of the house, banging the door behind him.

He walked to his room, took his tiny luggage, and headed for his girlfriend's residence.

***

"What! You're cheating on me with my best friend?" William remarked in disbelief when he came to his girlfriend, Lydia's home and saw her red-handed, having sex with John, his best friend on her sofa"

"And what is it supposed to mean? Didn't Lydia tell you we've been having an affair for a long time now?" John asked, leaping towards William.

What would happen to Lydia and what is Sandra preparing to do to William?

Chapter Four

"And what's it intended to mean? Didn't Lydia tell you we've been having an affair even before she met you?" John asked, leaping towards William.

William couldn't believe what John, his closest buddy had said. Lydia felt this was the ideal chance to let the cat out of the bag.

"William, I realize this may come as a shock, but it's true. I liked you since you were popular in school and affluent as well, but I never loved you.

I've been in love with John, even before you asked me out. I'm sorry I can't go through with the relationship anymore." Lydia stated confidently.

"Yeah, she's said it all. Though you are or should I say you were my best friend, you got anything you wanted, but you can never take my Girlfriend from me. She's mine, William.

Go find yours!" John said, facing William who had clenched his fists, shocked at what he just heard from his two most trusted friends.

William knew he'd lost this one but he wasn't going to walk away just like that, no way!

He went fast towards John and blasted him so hard on his stomach, forcing him to wobble backward and collapse on the couch.

Before Lydia could react, William delivered her a hard smack that made her fall on John.

John knew William was more strong than he was. Trying to fight William would be like a mouse trying to fight a lion.

So, they simply sat on the couch, staring at William and asking in their heart for him to leave.

"Fuck you back, stabbers! I detest you!" William stated. He glared at the two vulnerable lovers for a moment then rushed away, slamming the door so hard that it nearly fell off.

***

It was dark when William returned home and was greeted by Ruth, his nice old nanny, a middle-aged lady.

"William sweetie, welcome. I've been concerned about you" Ruth murmured as William went into the huge sitting area.

"I'm fine nanny. Where's mother and dad?" he inquired, absentmindedly.

"They traveled this afternoon. Thought you were aware" Ruth said.

"Oh yes! Mum told me, I forgot" William replied, suddenly missing his parents.

"Are you alright?" Ruth questioned William who was resisting the impulse to weep.

William understood there was no use keeping it away from a nanny whom he'd loved so much, even more than his parents.

William was fond of nanny Ruth. He respected and opened up secrets that he never disclosed to his parents to her since she cared for him and was always ready to listen to him and advise him.

"No nanny, I'm not fine. Why would I be alright when my parents do not even care about me?

All they do is travel every blessed day. They care about their businesses more than I. They don't even wanna know what I'm going through.

I chose to go see Lydia who I believed would help me forget everything I was going through at home, but what did I get? A heartbreak!

My girlfriend cheated on me with my closest buddy. Why has everyone decided to betray me, nanny?" William questioned, nearly in tears.

"Oh, dear! I am so sorry about it. I know how you feel since I was also deceived by the individuals that I trusted.

It wasn't easy getting over it, but I simply had to. William, you just have to try and pull through it, such is life.

Maybe you guys weren't made for each other. I think you'll meet another lady who's a hundred times better than Lydia" Ruth replied, rubbing William tenderly.

"Thanks, nanny. I need to rest, I'm feeling sick" William said, hugged his nanny, and walked upstairs to his magnificent room.

***

"Heard Lydia cheated on William with John," Linda remarked to Sandra and Lilian in class during break the following week.

"How did you know?" Lilian asked.

"Has anything ever transpired and remained a secret at Baverly High?" Linda asked.

"Poor guy! No surprise he's been silent and lonely these days" Lilian replied.

"Don't tell me you're pitying that thug! Remember I still haven't revenged him for nearly killing me the other day.

His girlfriend leaving him wouldn't stop me from following out my plan!" Sandra remarked, annoyed at Lilian's remarks.

"I'm not pitying him. But Sandra, I believe you should be cautious with the manner you go about your retribution.

He 'nearly' killed you the last time you revenged him and he may murder you this time around since he is already furious with everyone, everything" Lilian warned.

"Kill me? He can't do shit! I'm not terrified of him! I must get back at him, as a matter of fact, now is the greatest opportunity to attack, now that he is upset" Sandra stated.

William stepped into the class alone, and sat on his seat, looking forlorn.

"That's awkward! William comes to the class alone at the break. It's very unlike him who would jolly in the cafeteria with his pals or play volleyball outdoors" Linda murmured to Lilian and Sandra.

"Don't think I didn't hear that and don't think you can talk about me and get away with it!" William replied, stepping nearer the females.

Sandra stepped out of her seat and went to William, approaching him aggressively.

"And what can you do huh? Do you believe you've got everything in life thus you can bully whomever you want and get away with it? Wait, you think I'm truly terrified of you? No, I'm not, you weakly!

I honestly thought you were courageous until I watched you weep like a baby when your famous girlfriend deserted you for a better person, presumably because you've bullied her!

What are you waiting for? If you are man enough, go ahead and punch me! Pin me to the wall again!" Sandra said, boldly to the amazement of William.

William stopped motionless in amazement. Nobody has ever pushed him like this in his whole life.

He stood so near to Sandra and set his eyes on her boobs which were so huge and lovely. He knew precisely what to do to her.

Chapter Five

William stood so near to Sandra and set his eyes on her boobs which were so enormous and lovely.
He knew precisely what to do to her

Instead of hitting her, he grinned excessively

"You've got lovely boobs! But do something about your bra, the color is so faded, I'm forced to assume that's the only bra you've got.

You've scrubbed the crap out of that item, the pink tint has now gone to something else. You may now shut your buttons, I've seen enough" William murmured to Sandra, grinned at her, and went out, leaving her perplexed and stunned.

It was then that Sandra discovered that her two higher buttons were undone and her bra was showing. Ashamed, she immediately buttoned them, grumbled, and furiously marched back to her seat.

She didn't know who she was furious at in particular. Maybe with William for seeing her boobs and insulting her fading bra or maybe with her crazy buttons for falling open by themselves.

"Sorry about that, Sandra. At least you let him know you weren't terrified of him, that was very courageous of you. But how come your buttons were open?" Linda asked.

"Maybe they opened when she got up to confront William. Men, the guy's nuts! It's kinda funny. Sandra, please permit me to laugh!" Lilian remarked, laughing.

"I'm so gonna kill you if you laugh," Sandra said playfully.

The three girls fell back in their seats and began to laugh so hard that other students thought they were insane.

***

It was Saturday. Sandra decided she would go to the market this time around to acquire the items her mother would be needing to cook doughnuts that afternoon.

"Mum I'll be alright, I'm a big lady, I can't get lost in the market. Moreover, you've been the one going to the market every other day.

Please let me go today. Give me the list and go have some rest" Sandra pleaded to her mother who knew she would never cease the debate unless she gave in to her wishes.

She delivered the list to Sandra and advised her on how to go to the market.

"Please be cautious my kid. God bless you" Suzan replied, giving Sandra a brief kiss and waving her farewell.

***

"You need help, Ma'am?" Sandra questioned a middle-aged lady in the packed market after she had purchased everything on the list and was about to leave the market.

"Yes dear, I do need help. My car's parked outside the market and I'm finding it tough, bringing my things down there" The exhausted lady answered.

"I'll assist you, Ma'am, give it to me" Sandra offered, carrying the woman's weight until she came to where her vehicle was parked.

"Thanks so much, my daughter. You're such a kindhearted gal. What's your name?" The lady asked

"I'm Sandra"

"I'm Ruth," the woman said.

"Oh! Nice to meet you Ma'am" Sandra remarked.
"Same here dear. Please get inside the vehicle let me drop you" Ruth asked.

"Thanks, Ma'am" Sandra responded, sliding into the air-conditioned vehicle. Ruth got to know that Sandra could cook doughnuts.

"I adore doughnuts! Can't even remember the last time I took it. I'd want you to come to show me how to make it, would you, please?" Ruth asked

"Yes Ma'am, I'll gladly come over to teach you," Sandra remarked joyfully.

Ruth gave Sandra her home address as she left her off after complimenting her once again for the service she offered at the market.

***

"Mum I just made a new buddy. She's such a nice lady. Her name is Ruth." Sandra remarked to her mother when she returned home.

"Really? That's excellent" Suzan said, combining the flour and preparing to cook the doughnuts.

"Yeah. She said I should come to teach her how to bake doughnuts anytime I'm free" Sandra stated as she gave her mother the salt.

"Great! You may go this evening after we're done cooking" Suzan replied, beaming at her gorgeous daughter.

"Awwwn! thanks, mother! You're the sweetest mother in the world. I adore you"

Sandra murmured, embracing her mother who was preoccupied with mixing the flour.

"Love you too sweetie. Get me more water please" Suzan asked.

***

"Knock knock! Anyone home?" Sandra stated, on coming to the home address which Ruth provided her.

"Hold on! I'm coming!" A voice said from within.

While Sandra waited, her gaze wandered every inch of the gorgeous estate. From the gorgeous garden to the tranquil blue swimming pool.

"OMG!, Sandra, it's you! Please come in! So sorry I kept you waiting, was cooking" Ruth remarked when they arrived inside.

"No problem Ma'am. Mum sends her greetings" Sandra murmured, glancing at the neatly furnished home which smelled so delicious.

She set her suitcase on the chair and volunteered to assist Ruth in the kitchen. They spoke and joked continuously.

"So, now, to the real business. Let's get started. Can't wait to enjoy the doughnut, I think my son will adore it when he returns" Ruth stated

"I wish he does," Sandra remarked.

They were nearly finished with the frying when the doorbell sounded.

"That should be my boy. He's returned from the party he went to. Let me open the door for him, I'll join you in a minute" Ruth remarked and went to open the door.

William sweetie, welcome" Ruth replied, kissing William.

"Thanks, nanny. What's that delicious perfume that I'm perceiving?" William asked, salivating.

"An angel came over to tell me how to cook something amazing. Come to the kitchen and take a taste, you'll adore it!" Ruth remarked, enthusiastically.

"Alright. Can't wait to try it" William exclaimed, following Ruth to the Kitchen.

"What! What're you doing here, you bully?" Sandra questioned William in disbelief as he entered the kitchen.

"I should be the one to inquire what you're doing here since the last time I looked, this was my home!" William answered, similarly astonished.

What would be the consequence of Sandra at William's house?

Chapter Six

"I should be the one to inquire what you're doing here because the last time I checked, this was my home!" William answered, similarly astonished.

"Have you guys met before?" Ruth questioned, equally startled by them.

"Yeah, we're class buddy and..." Ruth stopped William who was going to inform her that this is the female who was constantly getting on his nerves.

"Wow! What a coincidence! William you never told me you had an angel for a classmate. She's such a nice, clever, charming, and intellectual girl with a wonderful heart.

If not for her, I don't know how I would've carried those hefty things alone in the market" Ruth added, gleefully.

"Oh! Nanny I need to clean up, I'm exhausted" William replied, his eyes firmly locked on Sandra.

"Thought you wanted to sample what we made" Ruth responded in surprise.

"Yeah... I mean no...em... I just lost my appetite" William stuttered, stunned at how gorgeous Sandra was.

He had never seen her in casual clothing before apart from school uniform. He realized that Sandra was much more beautiful than he'd thought.

She was an angel. The denim trouser she wore forced her butt to fly out and her small waist with her huge boobs gave her a complete curve.

Her flashing eyes may knock any weak person off balance. As William headed upstairs, his mind started to conceive something he realized he'd never imagined before.

He hastily pushed the insane ideas aside and made up his plan to ignore Sandra until she departs.

Sandra on the other hand found that the person she believed was a bully was not that rough at home.

He appeared quite attractive with a wide shoulder and long straight legs.

"Sweetheart, I sincerely appreciate your instruction. I'll start frying it myself from henceforth.

I'm sure William will love it when he eats it. Hope you'll wait and join us for dinner?" Ruth asked.

I wish I could, but I..."

"Please?" Ruth cut in.

"Okay, I will" Sandra answered faintly.

William came downstairs quickly to join Ruth and Sandra at the table for supper.

He sat immediately opposite Sandra who concentrated on her meal, trying not to glance at him.

"William, are you alright? You've been behaving oddly since you got back. Is something the matter?" Ruth broke the quiet.

"Huh? ehm no...nothing... I'm alright" William blurted out.

Ruth's phone rang. She answered it. She appeared upset after the call.

"Is everything okay Ma'am?" Sandra asked.

"So sorry kids, I've had an emergency. A buddy just phoned, informing me my sister is gravely sick. I need to go take her to the hospital.

It's seriously pouring outside, so William, you'll do me a favor by driving Sandra home in your vehicle when she's ready. Sandra darling, I sincerely appreciate your assistance. So sorry I won't be able to visit your mother as I anticipated. Send her my compliments and tell her I'll come to visit her once I'm chanced" Ruth remarked, gave Sandra and William a brief kiss, and departed.

As soon as Ruth drove out, Sandra's pulse began racing. She started to reposition awkwardly on her seat.

"Don't worry about getting me home, I'll find my way" she murmured, wishing her voice doesn't betray her.

"Find your path through the rain? Looks like the powerful queen is finally terrified of me!" William said, mockingly.

"I'm not, I'll not and will never be terrified of you!" Sandra replied boldly.

"Then why don't you want me to drop you? Do I have a lion in my car? Or you're worried your buttons are going fall open for me to view your boobs again?

Or are you irritated already that a disgusting and low-class lady like you is fortunate to share a meal with one of the wealthiest people in town?" William questioned, smiling in a manner that annoyed Sandra.

"How dare you disrespect me? I'd sooner delight, eating right from the gutters than spend another single minute with you. You may go ahead with your dinner, I'm out of here!" Sandra said fiercely.

She rose quickly, packed her dish and Ruth's, and headed swiftly to the kitchen. William stood up and followed her behind.

One thing about William was that he never said sorry anytime he was at fault, not even to Lydia while he was still dating her.

So he was thinking about how he was going to say an apology to a girl he believed he never loved.

"Sandra wait!" He murmured, as he entered the kitchen

"Yes? Go ahead, mock me! Insult me the way you like since this is your home! But you know one thing? I'll still be a nasty dream for you! I'll still detest you!" Sandra said.

"Really? You despise me?" William inquired, advancing near Sandra who moved backward until she couldn't go anymore due to the wall.

"Don't you dare get closer otherwise you won't like what I'll do to you" Sandra muttered, her back leaning against the wall.

"I'm so sorry Sandra, I can't stop" William muttered as if he was possessed.

"Don't you dare..." Sandra couldn't complete her final phrase when she realized she was terribly in his arms.

William kissed her lips hungrily. His heart pounded as if it was going to fall off his chest.

To his surprise, Sandra responded by kissing and caressing him back which made him moan in pleasure.

Nothing else mattered to him as he intensified the kiss, prompting Sandra to wrap her hands around his neck for support and then abruptly...

Chapter Seven

Nothing else mattered to him as he intensified the kiss, prompting Sandra to wrap her hands around his neck for support, and then abruptly Sandra took her lips away, pulling William back from the paradise of bliss.

Sandra couldn't do this. She would have been perfectly okay if this was any other guy, but of all the people in school, it was William who snatched her first kiss, what a paradox! She thought.

She knitted her hands together and blinked awkwardly, unable to get the words together. But she needed to ward herself after all.

"Just imagine this didn't happen since you can't bribe me with your kisses!" She remarked, almost in a whisper.

"Really? Sandra, why don't you just swallow your ego and admit that you're madly in love with me?" William questioned, putting his arms across his wide chest.

He didn't want this chance to go through his hands simply like that. So many crazy ideas flashed through his head while he watched her talk. He felt like eating her up, she was so sweet that only he would see it.

"In love with you? Don't let your thoughts fool you, I can never fall in love with a person who derives joy in harming me.

A person who nearly murdered me. A person who can't even say sorry when he's at fault. I can never fall for you!" Sandra said, looking William straight in the eyes.

William realized Sandra wasn't as easy as he thought she'd be. Any time he was at fault with Lydia, he'd kiss and romance her so that she'd forget he didn't apologize, but Sandra didn't forget.

"Would you at least give me your contact?" William asked, annoyed

"I don't have a phone and even if I had, I wouldn't give my contact to a bully" Sandra answered forcefully.

Why was she nasty to him, like she didn't have a moment with him some minutes ago? He had tasted her and had found out she was all hot for him, so why the pretense? He thought.

"Oh! So the almighty slay queen that has been making mouth all along does not have a phone at her age?

Are you so careless that you feel you won't be able to handle a phone or your parents don't trust you enough to give you a phone?" William questioned, forcing Sandra to recollect the unpleasant moment that led her to sell her phone.

Her mother was nearly beaten up by a lady whom she borrowed money from.

She didn't have a cent to pay back the irate lady. Sandra had to sell her phone to settle her mother's debt. Though she missed her phone, she was happy her mother was alright.

At least it was better to have peace of mind and avoid embarrassment than to have a good phone yet no peace of mind.

Sandra felt humiliated by William's words. She was sad and angry at the same time.

"You think you can talk down others because you have everything right? You may go ahead and utter whatever comes out of your mouth.

Go ahead and gloat, applaud yourself, you deserve honor as one of the wealthiest people in town.

You have a phone, a decent home, a vehicle and even a nanny to take care of you, but let me tell you something, you are not different from a pitiful beggar on the street.

Your buddies are striving to earn money, you are here talking about your father's money, shame on you, William.

You will only be a man if you know what it means to work. For now, you are a beggar with no choice but to accept where your father tosses you, rubbish!

I swear to God, if you dare come close to me again, I'll do something that will make you regret it for the rest of your life" Sandra said and stormed out of the house, not minding the heavy downpour or the scary thunder that struck as if it was going to pieces the angry sky.

William felt every word that Sandra said to him. Nobody has ever made him deep thought about his life. What kind of a girl was she? He asked himself.

"Sandra please wait, I didn't mean what I said please," he implored, but it was too late. She was out of sight.

***

Sandra was unwell when she reached home since she was wet from the heavy rain.

She couldn't go to school on Monday. She was shivering on the bed, even with the big cover on her.

Her mother was concerned. She went to pray when Sandra vomited the food and medications she gave her.

This was the type of era Suzan missed her spouse. If he was here, it would have been simpler for her since they would have had the money to send their daughter to the hospital for adequate care.

These thoughts made her cry tears since she was sad to watch her kid unwell but she couldn't assist her, she didn't have the money.

The money she earned from the doughnuts she sold was not enough, she needed more, but how was she going to acquire it? She thought.

***

Lilian and Linda realized something wasn't going right with Sandra since she had never stayed behind from school before.

William on the other hand was highly concerned and restless. Something told him Sandra wasn't fine.

What if she couldn't make it home? What if she fell sick as a result of the rain that drenched her? He thought.

He chastised himself for hurting her and letting her leave when it was pouring.

He realized he was hopelessly in love with this girl and he knew there were adjustments he had to make if he must have Sandra.

He'd have to confess when he's at fault and learn to apologize. He'd have to stop his pompous behavior.

He'd have to stop bullying people and he'd have to learn how to be caring for Sandra's sake, but will he be able to do all these for one person?

Tuesday, Sandra still didn't show up to school. William couldn't take it anymore.

He strolled over to Lilian and Linda who were afraid, dreading he was going to bully them because Sandra wasn't there to protect them.

"I'll report you to Principal Helen if you try bullying us," Linda said quickly when he got to them.

"Really? What makes you think I came to bully you?" William questioned, folding his arms.

"Because you're renowned for bullying virtually everyone in school," Lilian said.

"Well, someone helped me understand there's more to life than bullying. I don't bully anymore.

I didn't come to intimidate you guys, I came to ask for Sandra's home address" William remarked, calmly to the amazement of the two females.

"How confident am I that this isn't one of your tricks to damage Sandra?" Linda asked.

William felt unhappy. Has it gotten to this? He needed to turn a new leaf if he must be acquainted with Sandra.

"No, I promise I won't hurt her. I am just as worried as you are that she has been absent from school for two days." He replied in the calmest way he could.

"Fine. We were planning to go see her after school today, we're more worried about her " Lilian said.

William drove in his car with Lilian and Linda sitting quietly inside and wondering who could change him from a bully to a caring guy they never thought he'd be.

"Left please," Lilian commanded. William followed the girls' instructions attentively until they reached a tiny complex that contained a cottage with fading paint.

"Here is the home," Lilian replied, much to William's amazement. He assumed Sandra resided in a mansion.

They got down and walked inside the house. Suzan was sobbing in the sitting room.

She cleaned her eyes when they entered the room and welcomed them. She knew Lilian and Linda because Sandra had brought them home on several occasions.

When they asked her about Sandra, she narrated everything to them. She needed someone to speak to and she was pleased they came up.

"Ma'am please don't weep, nothing will happen to her. Where's she?" Linda inquired while William rubbed her softly.

"She's not here" Suzan answered, wailing more than before.

"Then where's she?" William questioned, nearly in tears.

Could Sandra be dead?
Would William forgive himself if it occurred that Sandra was dead?

Chapter Eight

"She's not here" Suzan answered, weeping even more.

Then where's she?" William questioned nearly in tears.

"She's in the hospital. I had to borrow money from my buddy and transport her to the hospital.

She has refused to eat for three days now and her condition is becoming worse since she's so weak, that she can't even walk without being assisted.

The money I received wasn't enough, so I came back to seek additional money, but I have no concept of how and where to acquire it.

I don't know what to do, I don't want to lose my only daughter. I'll murder myself if anything happens to her," Suzan remarked, still weeping.

"Ma'am, nothing will happen to her. Sandra will not die. Can we go visit her?" William asked.

"Yes, my children. Wait let me fetch the lunch I cooked for her, I'll take you there" Suzan replied, entering the kitchen.

William recognized Sandra was the carbon replica of her mother. Even with the grief on Suzan's face, the likeness was obvious. Tall, fair, and gorgeous exactly like Sandra. One could even mistake them for sisters.

***

They met Sandra asleep when they went to her ward. Linda and Lilian dropped some gorgeous flowers with a short letter written: "GET WELL SOON BESTIE, WE MISS YOU."

William simply stood there and gazed at Sandra who seemed even more gorgeous when sleeping.

He prayed quietly for her to wake up and hear him out, but his wish wasn't answered. She was sleeping until they went.

William had never felt this way before all during the years he had spent with Lydia and other females. There was something quite odd about Sandra that drew him like a magnet drawing iron.

He never anticipated that he was going to fall this deep for a lady he loathed some time ago. The worst of it was that he couldn't suppress the intense desire that was dragging him inexorably to her.

He thought about her all day and night. He hallucinated about her the day he got back from the hospital. She was gorgeous when sleeping.

He spotted her beautiful lashes, her gorgeous face, and fantastic skin. Her beautiful and juicy lips were so seductive that he envisaged kissing them again, this time, gently, releasing all the feelings within it.

William was physically unstable until his nanny saw it.

On Thursday, Sandra was finally released. William had paid her debts. He had urged

Suzan not to let her know he was the one who paid the bill. So she wasn't told.

***

"We're so thrilled to have you back. We missed you so much" Linda exclaimed when Sandra arrived back at school.

"I missed you too besties. Thanks for your nice presents and greetings" Sandra replied, beaming.

"En! Sandra do you realize that William is now a transformed person? He doesn't bully anymore. He even volunteered to take us to your home and to the hospital" Lilian stated.

"Kind of impressive, but that's none of my concern" Sandra answered.

She didn't tell anybody what occurred between her and William the day she visited. She made up her mind nothing was going to make her talk to him again.
She cautiously avoided him throughout the set.

"Sandra please wait. I have something to tell you," William remarked on Friday after school.

William had waited patiently for everyone to leave the class so he could pour out his feelings to her and this was a fantastic chance for him since he met her alone in the class, packing her books and ready to depart.

"Don't you dare get near to me, William. Stay away from me" Sandra said fiercely at William who was already confronting her.

"Sandra, I know I've wounded you so much. I know I'm the cause why you fell ill. But please, find a space in your heart and forgive me, I promise I will never harm you again," William implored.

"I've forgiven you. Can I go now?" She asked.

"No, there's one more thing. Sandra, you've transformed me entirely from the rough man who bullies and damages practically everyone to a person who thinks carefully before speaking or doing any action.

Baby, I'm madly in love with you. I've never felt this powerless before. Please make me the happiest man in the world by agreeing to be my girlfriend" William stated, staring Sandra directly in the eyes and wishing she gives him a favorable reply.

Sandra gazed at him. A lot of thoughts passed through her head. What if he only wanted to sleep with her and go, since he had had a taste of her lips?

She needed to be extremely cautious with him, she didn't entirely trust him, particularly for the fact that he used to be her bully.

"William, I would have liked to be your female friend, but it's simply not the correct thing to do. Moreover, we're about to start our final examinations and I wouldn't want to be sidetracked." Sandra answered.

William looked unhappy. But he still wanted to create a deep connection with this girl.

"Then can we be best of friends?" William asked

"Sure, I'm cool with it" she answered, smiling.

William got thrilled.

"Can I receive a hug from my bestie?" He asked. Before Sandra could speak, William embraced her so firmly, that her two legs dangled.

Since then, William and Sandra got quite close to one other. After school, William would drop Sandra at her house before returning home.

He became a regular visitor to her place. Sometimes, he would remain and observe while Sandra and her mother made the doughnuts. Suzan would give him to eat.

Each time William loses control and wanted to be intimate with Sandra, she would remind him of their agreement to remain the best of friends. William would get rid of himself, even if he was overwhelmed with a burning need to touch her.

Their friendship was strong till they graduated from high school.

They both chose the same University just as they agreed, though Sandra missed Lilian and Linda who were schooled outside the Country.

Everything went fine until William came to his last year. Sandra began seeing him with a certain female who seemed older and more gorgeous than she was.

Each time she faced William, he'd inquire if there was any issue. She'd grin and assure him there was no issue, after all, they were best friends, not lovers. But deep within her, she was feeling tremendously envious.

One Sunday evening, Sandra decided to pay William a surprise visit at his huge apartment. She felt even more envious of what she witnessed.

"Sandra! What a surprise! You never told me you were coming," William stated, letting go of the female he was romancing. The same female she had been seeing him with.

"Yeah, I wanted it to be a surprise visit, but I think I should get going since you are busy," Sandra said.

William sent the girl away and begged for Sandra to remain and she did.

Sandra couldn't contain the scorching need she felt for William anymore. She approached carefully to where he stood, looking at him like a hungry lion, ready to eat its victim.

Chapter Nine

Sandra couldn't contain the scorching need she felt for William anymore. She approached carefully to where he stood, looking at him like a hungry lion, ready to eat its victim.

"I know we vowed to be best of friends but I can't help but become envious each time I see you with that girl. It may seem odd to you, but I'm in love with you, William" She blurted out.

William's excitement had no limit. His fantasy had finally come true. He was not just infatuated with Sandra, he was hooked to her from the day he kissed her in his home.

He had hoped and dreamed that eventually, she'd feel the same way he was feeling for her and make his life whole since he felt incomplete without her. The bestie thing wasn't working for him, he needed more. He wanted her, desperately.

After dealing with his feelings for a long time, he decided to go seek nanny Ruth's guidance.

She instructed him to allow her time to discover herself, meanwhile, he could acquire a lady and pretend to date her, while studying Sandra's emotions.

If Sandra was genuinely intended for him, she'd grow jealous and come for him but if she wasn't, she wouldn't.

William was happy that nanny Ruth's counsel worked as anticipated. He grinned to himself for a job well done and glanced at Sandra who had matured from the innocent school girl he used to know to a lovely young woman. How time flies.

She looked lovely in her short gown, standing directly before him and expressing herself to him. He wanted to do everything for her, she was too lovely and he had waited so long for this time.

William couldn't bear the next second without the want to touch her.
He moved closer, his heart pumping extremely rapidly and loudly. He grasped her right hand and put it on his chest.

Sandra was startled by how rapidly his heart was pounding. He gripped her little waist and drew her to himself, peering deeply into her eyes. Sandra could see the fire in his eyes, she could interpret what they meant immediately.

"This is how my heart beats, each time I'm with you. You own my heart Sandra, you've always done.

I adore you with all in me. I've always loved you and I'll spend the rest of my life loving you if you give me the opportunity," William murmured against her ear.

Sandra put her face down again. She couldn't look at him because she was afraid she was going to do something foolish. He was too attractive. Too neatly constructed. His pleasant scent invaded her nostrils and she liked it.

"Look at me Sandra" William urged, holding her tightly to himself and raking his deadly eyes all over her. The type of glance that can sweep any female off balance.

"I can't. If I do, I'm worried I'll lose control and do something insane" Sandra answered.

"Please stare into my eyes and perform that insane thing to me. Anything you desire to do, sweetheart I'm all yours. Do it, I've been waiting and wanting all day for this"

Sandra gazed up at William who was anxiously waiting for their eyes to connect.
They locked up, peering into each other's eyes.

A tremendous spark of passion and closeness, immediately ignited as want raced through Sandra who suddenly behaved as if she was possessed.

She flung her hands around, William, pushing her soft breast to his chest. She kissed the corner of his lips softly. She then thrust her tongue in and he greeted her gladly.

William who was now gasping in delight, reciprocated and even took over the kiss, caressing her soft boobs.

The clothes she couldn't control anymore, he took her to the room and lay her on the bed like a baby.

He pulled off her clothes and his as well and did what he had been yearning to do since the day he fell in love with her. He caressed her until he decided to call his name.

"Make love to me" She murmured into his ear.

He moved down, pulled off her underwear, and issued her thighs. As if that wasn't enough, he sucked her and heard her groaning in delight. He went back to her lips and resumed kissing her.

"Please make love to me, you're killing me" she murmured again, terribly wet.

He grinned. He knew he had tormented her enough and he was going insane because he wanted her as much as she wanted him.

He filled her lips with his and just as he was ready to make love to her, there was a loud bang on the door.

THE END!!!

www.ingramcontent.com/pod-product-compliance
Lightning Source LLC
LaVergne TN
LVHW052049160826
845678LV00015B/3143

* 9 7 9 8 8 4 3 9 9 2 4 8 4 *